FORGIVEN LOVE

FORGIVEN LOVE

*For Those Couples in Love. Especially those Love
are never can be destroyed by any person in our
Milky Galaxy with any types of means.*

Ansley Andersen

BALBOA.
PRESS

A DIVISION OF HAY HOUSE

Balboa Press books may be ordered through booksellers or by contacting:

Balboa Press
A Division of Hay House
1663 Liberty Drive
Bloomington, IN 47403
www.balboapress.com.au
1 (877) 407-4847

Printed in the United States of America.

ISBN: 978-1-4525-2468-9 (sc)
ISBN: 978-1-4525-2467-2 (e)

Balboa Press rev. date: 07/03/2014

I am a current university student still studying. I got the second prize in short story competition in my final year of university. From then on I tell myself to write stories to provide humours to people.

Epigraph

Love is Love
Love not non-Love
Can we Love
Love to Love

PREFACE

This story is fiction dedicated to those have fallen in love, going to marry. Especially those married for a long life time without break-ups. Also to those love each other without grief or any regrets.

CHARACTERS IN THE STORY

Jennifer Elizabeth Kirby	main female character in story
Rolf Vincent Roland	main male character in story
Kaethe Kirstine Kaitar	Rolf's Mum
Eustace	Jennifer's dad
Shania	Jennifer's mum
Kenton Holt	Rolf's friend
Hanna Laurita Moore	Jennifer's best girl friend
Gabby	Hanna's dad
Marama	Hanner's mum
Firuz Holt	Hanner's boyfriend
Uncle Laurie	Jennifer's maternal uncle Shania's younger brother
Kabibe	Laurie's wife
Harrist Zaida Osbourne	Laurie's daughter
FACE	Federation of All Communities on Earth
FARE	Federation of All Races on Earth

CHAPTER 1

Love is love
Love is no wrong
Love what you love
Love is abundant

It is mid-Autumn in year 2639. I walk home after lessons. I, Rolf Vincent Roland and friends Madison Desmond and Kenton Holt in this chilly gusty afternoon. We are in the same grade for two years already. Madison is a quiet girl but Kenton is a gossip guy. All three of us are from poor families.

'Do you love wealthy boys, Madison?' Kenton asks.

'No. Actually there are no wealthy boys pursue me at this time.' Madison answers.

'Really, that is good.' I remark.

'Why?' Madison asks in wonder.

'Well, any boy has money, they play girls, big spenders and all playboys.' Kenton says.

'I do have some ideas on this topic. Frankly, why you two hate riches so much?'

Kenton is my best friend since we were in grade 1.We are now in grade 11. Kenton is only 19 years of age, I am 18 while Madison is also 19. Kenton and I both despised by riches since infancy. They increase our rental payment every year. We stay in the apartment under intolerable conditions. The apartment is small and dirty. No swimming pool and no gymnastics inside the building. The air-conditioning system is old and faulty pretty horrible. We expect delays and criticisms every time we seek for reparation. Fortunately we have a clean outside environment to reside. We all need to thank all those scientists 600 years ago to overcome the O-zone layer problem with cautions and wisdoms. That is why we now have cheap food while scientists are still working hard to create DNA human beings in a peaceful, intelligent and secure way to end up in a win/win solution to allow all sides are happy. When will they come to a success? It is hard to predict and foretell. We only can have fingers crossed.

Madison lives with her parents and three brothers while Kenton lives with his three siblings in the poorest suburb in Sydney. On my part I reside with my Mum while my late dad was dead two months after I was born. I am the only child in the family. My Mum and myself work pretty hard to earn for our living and my study. I wish I become Professor in Medical and Applied Science. But only Gold knows!

My Mum Kaethe Kristine Kaitar wakes up early in the morning to work part time returns home around 1330 hour. I also work part time 15 hours a week in a big departmernt store Memies. We both live happily together and refuse outside help especially my maternal and paternal relatives. We even do not disclose our residing address to them and they do not visit us neither even in Christmas nor at New Year.

Why we do this? Simple! Those relatives are monsters. They try every nasty method to ruin my Mum and myself. These mean people do whatever they are told from elders only to show they listen to parents and all are good boys and good girls. Hypocrites! Both sides of our relatives are garnish. They only keen on building up their own influences and power also lust for money. They turn to us when they are unhappy. Fortunately they are finally ignored by other riches and famous. God save the Queen!

Madison is a beautiful girl possessing a good body figure. All boys attracted by her figure in thirsty. Jesus! Maryson knows and refuses these playboys. They are the biggest losers. Madyson's ideal husband is a man has his own business and takes care of her. Madyson used to respect old people. She always tells us she is happy to take care of her parents-in-law. There is no doubt about that.

Madyson's beauty is absolutely incredible! Only at the age of 18 she is already a famous model in FARE. She already acted in a couple of movies with huge income award and pay lots of money in tax. Besides these Madison still works hard in her assessments. She hopes to become a medical researcher and theorist. A capable scientist to create better living environments and perfect human beings in FACE.

On Kenton's part this gossip boy loves Marketing. Inside his mind is all marketing principles and theories. The question is he is after two MBA titles then migrated to Venus to build up his marketing empire. He always promises to us even in wealth he retains all his promises to study and works hard in the meantime he retains purity in his family not to commit any single even tiny crime to destroy his family members and himself.

Kenton's idea is to build a better workable marketing system in Venus so as to establish mutual understandings between Venus and FACE. His framework is to introduce both cultures to the other planet residents to have a better and clearer knowledge of each other. To follow the good and peaceful characters of Venus people that hates wars and battles as to set up a better and more harmonies surroundings for both cultures.

Kenton is a smart man who researches on Venus past history and population customs. Kenton once told us he is going to marry a Venus girl when the time comes. Kenton loves their big and beautiful body figures the Venus people do not like travel thus, Kenton will do his best to persuade them to visit FACE at least once in their life time not many times. Alternatively, they watch FACE scenery, landscape and panorama from their digital watch computer which is Live from FARE.

On my part I, Rolf Roland, am a happy boy apart from those nasty non-human relatives. My Mum and myself live together in an apartment. We both have our own job. Sometimes I also work casual in Biotechnological Laboratory founded by a genetician 500 years ago. My work is a cleaner plus some hours on my own research but I have to report to management before and after my experimentation and exploration. Around 2100 hour I go home sometimes with a happy mood on the progress I just done on my own.

It is lucky I live in apartment building with my Mum. I can sometimes I can swim in the pool just next to our building. I am butterfly and freestyle lover and some backstrokes hoping to become champion one day. Hopefully! Both of us always retain a sturdy body. My Mum tells me 'every outstanding legend, man or woman, all stay in good health ready for their life-long battle in their career.'

My dreamed work is to complete DNA engineering work left behind by a famous scientist Oliver Manfort in year 2125. His work is fun and attractive and his innovations are next to perfect. This is my dreamed career!

CHAPTER 2

Spoiled child
Spoiled daughter
Spoiled not split
Still always together

The winter last year is horrible. Cold gusty winds all country around. Lucky for us there is no snow in Sydney area. It is not so fortunate for Snow Mountains. There are heavy falls of snowflakes and hailstorm. Residents overthere are expecting a coldest winter ever in history. Ice age is coming back?

The year 2640 is my turning point for the rest of my life. A new girl joins our grade 11 class together with some other boys and girls under the consent of our principal which no one knows why. People are talking about the new comers on their academic results can catch up with other students or not. Some bad students always curse they will end up in failure finally expelled from this High School.

The new comers catch up incredibly quick and some subjects they perform a pretty smart result than some of us. They come from Queensland or some from Victoria with a desire to do something for our Milky Galaxy. Some interested in astrophysics, some in nutrition and one loves war space ships engineering. One girl Jennifer Elizabeth Kirby is the most attractive in the group. She is beautiful with good body shape. Not too fat and not too thin, just right.

Jennifer wishes to become a scientist in medicine and some work on cosmology hoping to demonstrate the peace, harmony and sincere face of our FACE to foreign planets as to maintain a happy Milky Way Galaxy for ever. Why Jen wishes to be a medical researcher simply because many people in Victoria are easily infected by fatal diseases such as brain cell damage or reproductive system failure to produce healthy biological offsprings instead of produced by DNA Engineering.

Jennifer comes from a wealthy family. Dad is a well-educated famous philosopher on our FACE and a successful business merchant. Her mum Shania and her dad Eustace love her pretty much because Jenny is the only child in the family who finally becomes a spoiled child. This is why Jennifer behaves badly in classroom and in her private life. She thinks she is good at anything and beautiful since many boys madly chase her from her age of 15. It is true, absolutely true! Jenny's ideal husband is a person with good characters and home-oriented plus a challenging career. Can she find one? The truth is she is lovely, beautiful and intelligent and not multi-sexual lover.

Under my observation Jen listens to her mum's teachings. Shania has a fragile body with brain cell damage until now still under treatment. Besides these Shania is sure not to die at early age told by her neurologist. Thanks Buddha and God! Shania and Eustace deeply love each other. Eustace is busy during the day but definitely returns home for dinner and family gatherings. During weekends Eustace stays home preparing his business work meanwhile Shania prepares the meals. After lunch the whole family sit together or go to grandmother's home chatting and have fun. Eustace is a model father, son and husband. Everyone agrees. Shania is a good wife. No doubt! They have an ideal family that is dreamed by every single family inside FARE which is a peaceful utopia FACE for sure!

CHAPTER 3

Love comes
Bad goes
Really comes
Actually come

Thursday we are having our experiment with our own choice completed in laboratory. My friends' interests and mine are similar to research on amino acids and biotechnology. After work I go outside to have a break and fresh air in order to chat with other students. The topic we are talking is relationships between boys and girls. Suddenly someone screams. When we look back we find a girl Jennifer sitting on the lawn shouting, 'duck, duck, duck,,,,,,,,,,,,,,,,' and other coarse language.

'What are you saying, young lady?'

'I am telling you I am waiting impatiently!'

'What impatiently?' another boy shouts.

'Mind your own business, tard!'

'I have some businesses doing, frankly!'

'shut up you mustard.'

'Stop coarse language, lady.'

'Keep all your dirty mouths shut, boys.'

'You look like a tigress.'

'You look like a monkey.'

'Who is your man, betch?'

'It is confidential.'

'Girls have no secrets at this modern times.'

'Do you know you are not a girl?'

'I am partially a girl.'

'Oh God!'

'God won't save a girl like you.'

'God saves the Queen.'

'By the way, I am running out of cash to catch an air bus return home.'

'Good on you, mate!'

Jenny stood on the lawn talking to these students and now walking to bathroom angrily.

'Who is she?'

'She is Jennifer. A new school girl. Her family is friend of Principal. She studies overhere in order to get good results to go to university.'

'It is not fair. We study hard and now this girl butt in to have her share.'

'There is no share, mate. We all possess our knowledge in our minds. No share.'

'She is very arrogant.'

'Indeed she is. She is clever and a spoiled child.'

'I hate this type of girls, honestly.'

'It is not your choice. You have better pray to God.'

'I am Buddha follower, Sir.'

'Jesus Christ.'

Three weeks have passed all of us do the routine work as usual nothing changed and nothing is going to change. Wednesday Madyson comes to my workplace looked puzzled, surprised and ambiguous.

'She invites you to dinner.'

'Who's she?' I ask Madyson without knowing what is going on over that part of the world.

'J.......Jen........Jennifer.....'

'Jennifer?'

'Yes, Jennifer.'

'Jennifer Elizabeth Kirby?'

'Exactly correct. Jennifer Elizabeth Kirby.'

'Really?'

'Absolutely!'

'Buddha, please have mercy on me, PLEASE!!!'

'The dinner time is on Friday the following week at 1900 hour. Her address is 26 Mine Str......'

'Stop! I will not attend that dinner.'

'What's wrong, Rolf?'

'Nothing wrong but now I do not want to know this girl.'

'She is alright.'

'We are not in the same world. Her family is rich but I come from a poor family. After we get married her friends are going to gossip our relationship. At that time her parents cannot cope with this situation then she is under pressure to divorce. Why get married at the first hand?'

'Optimistic, Rolf.'

'This is not the core reason. I hate her because of her arrogance. This is certain to cause problems in the family.'

'Why not give it a go, Rolf?'

'No go is good go I suppose.'

'Come on, Rolf!'

'Please decline her offer on my part, Madysen.'

'It is all up to you.'

In the following few months I do not see Jennifer Elizabeth Kirby in College. Maybe she avoid me, God knows! Examinations finally come. All our candidates are promoted to university and I heard that Jennifer becomes first in her class.

I commence my university study smoothly going to Medical Genetics and Philosophy Theory and Practice. Kenton is first in all units in his Marketing Degree. Madysen is cute too she always stays on top 3. Why they are so smart? No one knows. Am I able to find out the reasons on my research? Hopefully.............!

CHAPTER 4

Study or work
Work or study.
Business or recreation
Life Life

New semester is going to start in a fortnight. I am highly alert to wait for this, honestly. In the Summer Vacation Kenton went to Galenain City in Venus to look for chances of his career out there while Madysen went to Western Europe former country of Croatia, Croatia-Hopenny Republic to earn her fashion model business in return of 3 million bucks as bonus.

Kenton's Galenain City tour was pretty successful. He found out the areas of marketing he can work on which makes him pretty excited. Besides this, he met a beautiful girl in a small town in northern hillside district of Cuppaboy City. The city is close to capital Motherland. The girl he met is so charming that, as he describes, much more beautiful and better than FARE girls he has seen ever.

Kenton also told another story happened in Universe [that is university on earth] in Motherland. There was a student in Universe studying "Inter-Galaxy Legal and Theory, current and future" degree. The student did not have high marks in assessments and examinations also did not pay attention in lectures. One day he was chatting with the student sitting next to him. This student, Smit Ved Smithe was talking happily interrupting the Lecturer. The Lecturer was so annoyed he threw Smit Ved Smithe out of the lecture theatre and said to him, 'Don't ever come back to all my units!' All students clapped hands and cheered because Smit Ved Smithe was a nasty student always caused troubles.

When Smit was outside he persuaded other students went on strike targeted to stir up hatred between lecturers and undergraduates. After hearing all these some students were so frustrated they reported to Universe Security Department. At last, Smit was sent to police station by Universe authority jailed two years then executed under Venus Criminal Legislations of Social Security.

On my part I am not so lucky. I worked three day week to earn sufficient money for my semesters. On other days I stayed home reading eBook, research and stayed with my Mum. The three day work is easy. Prepared equipment for experiments and the cleaning job. Looking at the scientists busy on their theory experiments to me is amazing. They are good scientists busy on looking to compose benefits to people upon their innovations.

Besides work I went to shopping to purchase daily essentials to bring back home. On my part I rather stay home chatting with my Mum in our own paradise. Mum always teaches me Buddha principles which I learn by heart. Mum and i go out for dinner, to beaches and cafes watching the oceans. Sky, stars and people walking by. Sensations! I honestly love it. When I am alone I brainstorm my science research theories. On Sundays we watch movies from the computer-movie home cinema. What a splendid vacation!

This morning before lecture I met my friend Leisa. A medicine student graduating at the end of this semester Leisa is pretty talkative always bla, bla, bla.......never stops.

'Good work, Leisa. You are the happiest girl in town in May graduation.' I said.

'Thanks, Rolf. Frankly, I have done a lot of hard work on study. days and nights. God!'

'Seriously?'

'You are also an undergraduate on your own. You should have experienced the bitterness and hardships, should you not?'

'I understand.'

'God!'

'We all need to work and study hard, otherwise, we are in deep trouble.'

'In those study years no one knows my burdens and sufferings but myself.'

'I share with your experience, mate.' I said.

'Lucky for me, I still can graduate in May despite some failed units during my training.'

'What is your next step?'

'Go to practice and further education.'

'Which area?'

'Cardiology, hopefully!'

'Good on you, Leisa.'

'I appreciate. I badly need that.'

'What are your favourites in Medicine degree?'

'Well! Nothing unusual.'

'What is that "unusual"'

'When patients come. General Practitioners prescribe medication to let them recover.'

'It is a lot of knowledge.'

'Not necessarily, actually.'

'Why?'

'Only need to give medicine for that virus.'

'How does it go?'

'To stop virus infection.'

'Then?'

'Then if it does not we are finished.'

'Finished?'

'Yes, finished.'

'What?'

'We have no other options.'

'Any chances?'

'None at all.'

'That means patients can only recover at random.'

'Absolutely.'

'God!'

'Only God can save you!'

'Jesus Christ!'

'Viruses can mutate some medicines. It is our job to provide new vaccines all the time.'

'And then?'

'And then we have a new weapon.'

'A new weapon?'

'Yes, a new weapon.'

'Are you trying to tell me patients are at all risks once when they are sick?'

'Obviously.'

'Buddha please help me.'

'You need to have a healthy body, mate.'

'I need it. I really badly need it.'

'Yeah!'

'Doctors are wealthy people then.'

'Hopefully right!'

CHAPTER 5

Time comes and goes
Things start and end
Is it Life
What is Life

This morning I wake up early ready for University. It is a chilly morning. In century 25 scientists tried to control weather but did not succeed. Then they turned to lessen storms and floods severity by keeping concord with natural weather conditions. This is what they have done! When there is storm and draught the weather conditions will change to mild and chilly. Whenever there is storm weather scientists will manipulate scientific technology to drive the storm back to oceans. Cool and cosy weather is what we now have for over 100 years.

It is because there was no rain yesterday most of the town residents ask for rainy conditions till March, Autumn comes. I therefore, catch air bus to study at Townsville Bus Stop. I arrive campus to see many students are already there. I greet my friends and former classmates. They say 'Hello' to me and I reply 'Hello' in return. They smile at me I smile at them. What is it?

When I come to Lecture Theatre there is only a few students inside. When Professor comes we are all surprised because it is Professor Roderick Hudson. Same Lecturer of astrophysics last semester who, most students think he is an intelligent ape and all give him a 'Yes' confidence vote since he is a model Lecturer. He conducts lecture in a simple, easy to understand study materials and no ambiguity in study blocks plus no repeat and repeat and repeat on theories. He used to not teaching astrophysics but astrobiology. Why? We all have no cues. What a headache!

After lecture I am preparing back home. Suddenly I hear someone calling my name behind me. I turn my shoulder only to find out the caller is Jennifer. Yes. Jennifer Kirby. She is calling my name while she runs towards my direction.

'Hi, Rolf, not seen you for a while. How are you going?'

'Standing in front of you is really a hazard.'

'Come on Rolf. Don't be narrow-minded and stubborn please.'

'No one can read my feelings, honestly.'

'Hey, Rolf I come over talking to you because we are friends. But I am assaulted by you every time.'

'Because you are ugly. You do not look like a girl. You are omen suddenly come down to earth.'

'Rolf, could you mind your tongue?'

'What?'

'Behave yourself you bestard. Always show off your intelligence but fortunately get low marks every examination.'

'This is my business. Betch!'

'What you shat!'

'None of your business.'

'I try to invite you in a polite manner but you do this to me!'

'I do what I like. This is my way!'

'That's why my dad told me you are a person as stubborn as a donkey.'

'I appreciate your appraisal, mate.'

'Rolf, you are a mean person. Mean means always mean.'

'I am happy at this stage.'

'I really regret to come over invite you to my family dinner.'

'See you!'

'Fortunately I do not wish to see you again. Bye, Rolf the wolf.'

Next thing I am going to do is to the Lab.. I maybe 30 minutes late, Jesus, that beech! When I am in the Lab. I cannot concentrate on my work. I always deviate to other directions. I can't handle, I can't cope with this situation, I can't, lord!

Jennifer is driving her Heep XXXVI vehicle back home. In the car she sobs, pretty pitiful! Her mind always appears the scenes she just had with Rolf, she is so unhappy..............

'Hey, what are doing?'

There is nearly a crash. Jennifer abruptly focus on her driving. All matters are decided after she is safely home.

In Jennifer's bedroom Jenny lies on her bed sobbing, sobbing quietly and sadly. Suddenly,

'Jennifer, are you OK?'

'Yes mum.'

'Are you right?'

'I am fine, thanks mum.'

'It is time to look for a new boyfriend, young lady.'

'No, no, no. I love him all my life. Honestly, I love him from the bottom of my heart.'

'Silly girl! All has passed.'

'Mum please tell me what to do next?'

'Virtually not let you dad knows. He always objects you know Rolf. He is no good. Why he despises Rolf? Poor fellow!.'

'Mum could you please explain to dad?'

'I try my best, Love. But I can't promise, you know. Every time you talk to him ends up in quarrel. He is pretty arrogant.'

'That's the problem.'

'It is because he comes from a wealthy influential family. Born to be rich, raised up in rich. Jesus, he promised me to be humble after our marriage. He does change a lot but why he insists on this matter? Maybe no one knows!'

'Is there something unusual?'

'I suppose there is something wrong.'

'Where?'

'I have no idea! We will find it out anyway.'

'Mum, at that time it is too late. Rolf may have married another girl already.'

'Don't be silly, girl. If it belongs to you, you will always possess it for the rest of your life.'

'That means there is a slime of chance he is mine or I become a step mother?'

'Good point.'

'What am I going to do now?'

'Try to work out why he hates you. Find out the real truth.'

'What means?'

'Try Madison. She is Rolf's best friend. She might have some cues. Or Rolf's mother. Rolf is a good boy he used to listen to his Mum.'

'Make it happen then!'

'What to do?'

'It is a good idea to apply a job in her workplace. You know her then you can talk to her persuade her to make her change her mind and then pull her to your side.'

'Really?'

'Yes really and seriously.'

'If it does not work?'

'seek help from your best friend.'

'Hanna Laurita Moore?'

'That's my girl!'

Jennifer visits Hanna the next morning only to find out Hanna has gone for vacation and returns on the 23rd of the month that is two days from now. Jennifer has nothing to say but return home. It's all tough luck, God!!!

On Monday morning 26th February Jennifer goes to University in a chilly weather without delay. When Jennifer is on campus she goes straight to Science Faculty to look for Hanna. Jennifer has come to study in the same University as Rolf. But Rolf has not a single cue all the way. Hanna and Rolf are partners in laboratory sessions. Both done a good job that they get very high marks in academic results.

'Hanna.'

'Oh! Hi Jennifer.'

'How are you?'

'You give me an astonishment just now beautiful girl.'

'Hopefully not a bad experience.'

'I was told you visited me a couple of days ago but not come back on the 23rd.'

'I had dizzy on that morning, to be honest.'

'Still under depression?'

'Oh! Baby.'

'No worry, all will be right, hopefully.'

'How was the vacation?'

'A good experience! I went to Mars on my own. On this red plane it is a hot and sultry planet you can't find one place in our Milky Galaxy to match it, to be honest. You see I come back with tan colour. Worse than back from Africa.'

'Who recommended to visit Mars?'

'My boyfriend, stupid'.'

'This is a good reason not to listen to boys under any circumstances even after marriage.'

'I really have a lesson in my life.'

'My God! You are a fast pick-up fellow.'

'Perfect.'

'By the way, can you do me a favour?'

'Of course what a stupid question.'

'Thanks a lot first.'

'What is the problem, honey?'

'Frankly, I fall in love with a guy in your same degree. His name is called Rolf but he does not talk to me. I wonder do you have any tips to change Rolf's mind to let him stay with me for the rest of our lives?'

'This is a big trauma to be certain.'

'Please!'

'Well, I will do my best. Why Rolf not talking to you?'

'I honestly have no idea.'

'Okay, no matter what. I know Rolf is looking for a girlfriend for a long time. The girls…..'

'Has he found a sweetheart?'

'Not really. He is expecting Gamma but his mother has a bad impression on Gamma. Lately people said they already broke up'

'What a pleasant gift, God! Why his mother does not like Gamma?'

'Gamma is pretty arrogant and not good to Rolf's mother. That is why Rolf……………'

'Goodness me!'

'All is in a strangled. Any way I promise to help you but don't let him know. Otherwise I lost a good work colleague.'

'OK.'

'OK, deal.'

'Deal with fingers cross.'

After this conversation Jenny does not see Hanna in her home or on campus. Jennifer thinks Hanna might have evaporated to a tiny morning dew. But suddenly one morning Jenny receives Hanna's call ask her to come to Hanna's home for dinner the following night without delay. Jennifer also told she will be expecting to see Rolf as he is the only guest besides Jenny. Jennifer is so delighted that she tells her mum straight away as her mum tells Jenny not to let her dad know. Why and what is it?

At dinner night Jenny is the most attractive girl in the party. Rolf is late because of heavy traffic from Blue Mountain where he is trained for hospital work experiences. He is happy to stay there for 3 days. When Rolf arrives he is puzzled to see Jennifer there. Rolf says nothing but only talks to Hanna and her mother and father, Marama and Gabby. Then retreats to dining table quietly. During the night all are chatting happily only Jenny and Rolf stay silence. Jennifer always look at Rolf with a blushed face and Rolf looks at Jenny from time to time secretly. Still both do not talk to each other. What's happening? God knows!

After dinner Rolf finds a pretext to go home early while Jenny has early morning university commitments brings Jenny to leave 15 minutes after Rolf's departure. Back home the couple does not have a good time. Both turning on bed cannot go to sleep. The vivid dinner scene seems in front of their eyes. He is a handsome man and she is a charming girl. She is pretty but possesses too much wealth. Once Rolf stroking in front of her home coincided her father Eustace came back from work. Eustace praised Rolf was a smart boy only to recall his business counterpart told Eustace Rolf was a gaol at age 15. Eustace hurry expelled Rolf and was ready to grab a tree branch to hit Rolf's head. Fortunately, Rolf ran away as fast as he could in his life time.

Whenever Rolf re-thinks this scenario he is pretty annoyed but without saying a word. By the way, what is Jenny thinking now? She recollects Rolf's beautiful face, recognises his talent and humour. Jenny has sometimes heard her friends saying Rolf does not love her money but indeed Jenny does not know the incidence Rolf had with Eustace. Jennifer is not mean, not prejudice nor narrow-minded. The question is why Rolf does not talk to her? Why, why and why?

Chapter 6

Love comes
Love goes
Loved one comes
Loved one goes

Back to my study we have 2 lectures on each unit already. What I am doing now is to set down a timetable for both study and work. I am pretty happy to return to study after Christmas vacation. On these two days I heard rumours that Professor Patron is having his retirement in middle of August this year. What a horrible news! Many of us wish to find out the reason but failed. Recently there is an announcement on notice board proves it is true. The notice invites all staffs and students to participate in a farewell party in early July right after semester examinations.

Professor Gero Patron is already 95 of age. He worked hard in his school life to go to university. After 5 years of bitter study in Double Degree Gero is the first undergraduate to obtain full marks in every test and all examinations over the five long difficult years. Is there any secrets on anatomy and physiology inside his brain? It is certain we must ask God!

Gero got his Professor title after he completed his research on human brain cells. In his work he found out those parts for deduction, memory and to encode or decode, functions of neurons and electric signals in brain communications. His work was so amazing that opened a new era of neurological research and debates because of his research results could answer over 50% of unknowns at current stage.

Upon Gero's remarkable discoveries do not let him to become arrogant. On the contrary, he is still a humble man who never ever shows off only occasionally goes out to sea to enjoy pleasure of nature ends up like an African black giant on his return.

Gero still wishes to continue with his research. He is convinced by Vice-Chancellor he can work in laboratories on campus. Gero is having another breakthrough on brain cells functions. Different body parts send different types of electric signals to each other to communicate. These different signals are derived from different genetic codes. Some scientists criticise this proposal arguing there is no fundamental proof. Therefore, Gro works hard with his team to prove they are correct. Are they correct? No one knows!

It is now winter time June 2643. I have all my examinations completed. What I am going to do now is to wait for final graduation examination at the end of the year to pass. Hopefully! On the following day I receive a call from Hanna telling me Jennifer's father was dead for one month. Now Jennifer is staying with her mother at home. Jennifer's mother is managing her husband's business and seems going smoothly. Her mother Shania wishes to invite my Mum and myself to dinner Friday night next week. I excuse myself by saying I need to talk with my Mum before gives Hanna a reply. Hanna says nothing but to hang up.

Two days later I ring Hanna to say we are going to dinner on that night. After a few hours Hanna rings back only to tell me Jenny is the happiest girl in Sydney when she received this good news. On that night Hanna goes to dinner in the same air vehicle with my Mum and myself. Inside the vehicle Hanna is pretty talkative always gossips. What she is talking is to arouse my attention. What are these?

I honestly have no idea. Who can tell me? How about you, folk? Oh god, how are you? Don't ask me please! On the way Hanna and her mum, Marama always praise Jennifer is a good girl. They always say this to see my Mum's response. My Mum is pretty happy as to ask Jenny's details especially her attitude towards elder people. They are chatting gladly when we arrive our destination.

CHAPTER 7

Delicious food
Are delicious people
People need food
Food are delicious

We are greeted by Shania at the front door. Shania is really courteous that she talks to my Mum non-stop. Marama and Hanna say "Hello" to Shania and start to talk to Jenny. Only myself is left alone. Then comes Jenny to invite us to go inside. The house is beautiful but not pretty large. Nowadays you cannot find a house or apartment occupies hundreds of square metres. On FACE or FARE there are more than 100 billion people staying at this time of year. Our earth is a tiny planet while our President of FARE always encourages people move to other planets. By this we can establish friendship among planets on multiculturalism to share opinions and maintain harmony in this Milky Galaxy.

There are five rooms or small rooms in the house. They are double-bed rooms altogether 3 rooms, a kitchen, a dining room, a swimming pool outside and a modern laboratory for Jenny's research. All places inside the house are amazing. They are well-designed to make the most of it.

In each room there is a broadcasting system, a mimic system to be honest. Jenny has her own study desk in her bedroom. Whenever

Jenny works out some theories she will go to the lb to verify even works up to dawn. Jenny's mother is a Catholic thus so is Jenny. They have a prayer room or to say a mini church. Everything you can find in a Catholic Church you can also find it in their prayer room. Shania named this room as "Our All Mighty Lord Room". In the mornings Shania prays in this room after Jenny has gone to campus. Now Shania's only hope is on Jenny. Jennifer will have a good husband and a good career no matter under what circumstances. This is the only reason Hanna and her family helps them from the very beginning. But again Jenny and Hanna are good friends same as both families. Before Jenny's father died Eustace wished to visit the Vatican City at the end of 2043. Then tour planet Mars on their return. But now these are bubbles, hopeless dreams. No father, no husband and no planet. But Shania and Jenny are happy what they are now. Frankly, Jenny does not like travel as well as Shania who cannot sit in space travel ship for a long time because of osteoarthritis after marriage. Jennifer prefers to work from morning till late at night then comes home stays with Shania in their own paradise. She does not lust for reputation nor even power. Her only wish is to become a scientist or let's say a pretty able and capable scientist to work for needies in our Milky Galaxy. But can she? Shania always prays to God to let Jenny accomplishes her goal meanwhile Jenny really works pretty hard, not lazy, in every moment she has. Let's see!

One more room needed to mention is the sports room. Jenny like other Sydney girls is fond of netball. Thus, in this sports room there is a netball playground, small but modern to allow any netball games. Jennifer practises netball techniques and fundamental exercises then jogging for another 10 minutes everyday before commence work. No excuses.

Even on this modern Earth we can travel from planets to planets. These ancient sports retain its form and pattern through ages under its past glory. There is no doubt about it. My God!

When Hanna talks to me before dinner. I tell her I am pretty excited on the final graduation examinations. Because after this I can apply for jobs and still stay on my laboratory research.. as I am talking I become more and more excited, nervous and happy in such a loud voice that suddenly Hanna shouts, 'Good on you. Are you alright?' God!

On Hanna's part she is also looking for jobs in veterinary section which includes any type of animals but not Human Beings in other parts of Milky Galaxy. Honestly speaking, Hanna always tells me she is lazy and she is ugly. It turns out she always stays with furry animals such that no matter where she is that Hanna is always the most beautiful girl in her boyfriend's eyes, Firuz's mind.

Firuz is a Galaxy Event Organiser [GEO]. As he is working on this job Firuz needs to have challenging ideas to take part in any big performances any time anywhere. He always shows people interested events on air from planets to planets to help the tourist industry especially on his own business benefits. On the contrary, Hanna has her secret framework. She plans to work part time in an animal's hospital in the meantime she studies part time on "Animal Science" in university. This is a good schedule. She can study and earn her livings at the same time. Can she balance work and study is another question!

Of course she can! Hanna sets a timetable on work, study and rest plus activities in short break periods. She tries hard to balance these three different episodes. She is eager to succeed with any price.

Dinner time comes. The courses are delicious and yummy that no one says no good particularly Hanna's mother Marama. The dishes are monkey brains, Mars roast hares, Venus deep ocean oysters, reddish brown octopus and calamari. Deserts are Saturn grapes, planet Roome and Earth hybrid apples, Mars hybrid berries and plums. Finally, Venus blue spicy tea. Sounds good! All people in house are talking to one another about the dishes even the following few days. At dinner table adults talk to adults while boys and girls talk to boys and girls. It is the first time Jenny talks to Rolf face to face.

'Rolf, not seen you for a while. How are you going?'

'Well, quite good. Thank you.'

'Quite good? What were you doing in vacation?'

'Earn my livings, hanging around and do business to make some profits.'

'That's a lovely idea! What business did you do?'

'It is small business. Besides it is my final year, I do my best to pit my hand on investments on FACE.'

'What investments?'

'It is small investments. My main career is my science profession. If not why I spend so many years to study this Bachelor degree?'

'Apart from work do you have any thoughts on other interested zones?' Such as family life and your future life?'

'I have a pretty good family life. I stay with my Mum. We both work, we eat and go out together and we talk to each other. We earn our own livelihood to expend in our own way.'

'What happened to your friends?'

'They are good. We help each other on our study. participate in camping,swimming carnivals, tennis contest and others.'

'I heard many people say you always leave early in public occasions. Why?'

'Yeah, I prefer stay home to dine with my Mum instead of those gatherings.'

'Why not eating outside?'

'Whenever I eat outside I rather go with my Mum, my children and my wife not other people but my only best friend.'

'But why?'

'I do not wish to take in delicious food without my Mum. I won't let her only take in simple food without nutrition. I am certain these are going to ruin her life.'

'That means..............'

'Whenever I am in poverty. I still stay with my Mum not to beg others to help us. When I am wealthy I am sure to share with my Mum and my wife. That is my own family.'

'Yeah! Good…….good……'

'Do you have any girl friend?'

'Not this stage.'

'Any girl you want to talk to when you are in depression?'

'There is and there are but I honestly do not know she listens to me or not.'

'Really?'

'Yes for sure.'

'How about talking to me?'

'I will try but why?'

'I love listen to your philosophy and code of conduct.'

'It puts burdens on me.'

'No, I don't think so.'

'Maybe you don't understand.'

'Not understand what?'

'You are still young.'

'What for?'

'Young and inexperience.'

'This is your opinion.'

'Serious?'

'This is what you see and what you think.'

'These are nonsense.'

'Well ……..'

'Don't always keen on what you think. Do have a second thought.'

'You are a good son look after your Mum pretty pretty good.'

'I have to.'

'Why?'

'My Mum has a pitiful life, no one in this world is a good person to do favours to her. Even her husband, a nasty hypocrite, betrays her and insults her. She cannot stay in this situation for the rest of her life. She must enjoy her life which she is happy for at least another 30 or 50 years.'

'Are you sure?'

'I stand firm on this. I say it I mean it.'

'How about your wife and children?'

'I wish my wife also treats my Mum good and my kids respect their paternal grandmother. In return I do best to my wife's parents and family on conditions they are lawful, ethical and accepted by society on a good conduct to serve all parties to have a win/win solution.'

'Sounds great!'

'Besides I wish my wife is a good wife who helps in my business and research career, a good daughter-in-law and a good mother.'

'Om …. Om….'

'If my wife harms my mother the only option is divorce.'

'Oh! No, not this.'

'I can tolerate my wife's legal wrongs to other people but not my Mum. This is already a step back to save my marriage.'

'Oh! I see.'

'I honestly do not wish my wife does any wrong. But who knows? You cannot foretell there is storm and tornado is coming tomorrow. Can you?'

'No, I honestly can't.'

'I am prepared not to marry in this current life time. What is the point to get married to end up a snake wife plus a broken family?'

'I agree.'

CHAPTER 8

Good consequence
Really is it not
Cape of Good Hope
Really is it not

Early in the morning adults go to work children go to study as their routine life. By now what are Jennifer and Rolf thinking of? Jennifer is a good girl. Rolf is an intelligent science student. But what? Jennifer genuinely loves Rolf. This is 100% correct. But what about Rolf's attitudes on this? Does he care? Does he mind? Does he consider as a concern? Who knows? Except Rolf himself.

On the air bus Rolf falls asleep because he could not go to sleep the night before. Only 2 or 3 hour sleep. Suddenly,

'Rolf, wake up, wake up. Quick.'

'Eh, who is it?'

'I am Jennifer.'

'Jennifer? What are you doing here?'

'What are you doing here? We should get on shuttle bus to uni.'

'Where?'

'Oh God! Are you Okay?'

'I am OK.'

'What are you doing today?'

'I purchased hybrid turkey and duck back home.'

'Oh God! You are going to campus.'

'Yeah! I am on my way.'

'Are you sure you are OK?'

'I hope so.'

'Let us get off this bus now. Hurry !'

'Jennifer, I am going this way.'

'Alright, join me in the lake down under at 1500 hour.'

'Maybe.'

'What are you talking about? Maybe.'

'I need something.'

'What is that?'

'I honestly have no idea.'

'I know, you need a family.'

'Perhaps.'

'Whenever you are happy or blue, come over.'

'Alright bye.'

At two o'clock Rolf needs to complete his lab experiment for another one hour and a half. Can Rolf keep his appointment? Who knows! Jennifer is heading to lecture theatre to attend lecture. Her watch rings and a message is left over. In that afternoon Rolf does not go to the lake instead Jenny stays there watching the sky and sun up to half past four heading home with tears in both eyes.

'Jenny, you are back!'

'Oh! Uncle Laurie, not seen you for a long time. Where have you been?'

'I went to Jupiter to research on natural resources to come to a profitable method for business.'

'Good work! By now you have already done it?'

'Not really! Ah, almost completed the report. We are still waiting for a reply from authority.'

'Laurie, stay overhere tonight. We go out for dinner, shall we not?'

'Good idea!'

They go to a restaurant, Idol Love Healthy Food Restaurant,t near Coogee beach at 1823 hour. The courses are delicious. Shania talks to Laurie all the time. Laurie Kirby talks about his program "Natural Super-Light Zone Gases" which is standing by for Jupiter authority to approve. Is it a benefit arrangement? No one knows. Only wait and see.

At this moment Laurie's wife Kabibe stays home ready for the medication for her seasonal flu. Meanwhile Kabibe still takes care of her daughter Harriet Zaida Kirby who had a big fall resulted in a broken knee. Harriet had a surgery on splice and reunion of her knee from her own stem cell. Now she is healthy and fit as before. Do you believe in this?

The restaurant is fully owned and functioned by a Mars migrant Aai Beich Cabesto. Aai employs a super chef Ichior Hadad Robinson who cooks European Union food is rule of the thumb. That's why they have big profits every year. Ichior Hadad Robinson earns huge commissions to invest on property market and food research industry. Can it be true?

The party orders dishes of ancient European kings and queens favourite foods. Jenny listens to music while Shania and Laurie talk to each other rather enjoying the food. They chat non-stop. So much to gossip? It looks like they are old friends departed for more than 30 years. Not supposed by other people they are actually brother and sister.

Jenny sits and listens to the chat because the music in restaurant she has heard before via digital—watch-tv-computer-system. These are hit songs and stay on top 200 in global contest for five weeks. At current situation people wish to compose a song they need to complete Master degree of Music [MM] before writing songs and lyrics. The song needs to be memorised easily in order to sing with emotions. The singer in this restaurant is also a song writer. He is only 20 years of age. He already can play 5 different musical instruments. Who knows the hardships and sufferings he has during his training.

Reminic's voice is soft and he is able to sing high key notes loud, strong and clear. He can sing any types of songs even performs in opera.

Frankly, he is a gifted singer possesses nearly all the requirements a singer should have. Who know what happens next?

The dinner meal takes more than three hours. In the air vehicle Jenny is so compassionate by the lyrics together with her current situation that she sobs. Shania calms her down without success. Poor Jenny cannot go to sleep that night. This little girl is still thinking why Rolf does not pursue her. She is not stupid. She is hardworking. She is a good girl at home and in school. She is beautiful. She is considerate and concern. She hates devils and stubborn criminals. It is logical. She never ever cheats. Also she has no discrimination attitudes. Why Rolf does not love her no matter what methods Jenny uses to grab his attention. Why? I don't know why.

The following night Jenny is sound asleep. In the morning it is Thursday week Jennifer does not need to go to campus. Jenny revise her study on Medicine then works on research for better human characters under new DNA functions. This is a controversial science topic. Some parts on Earth have banned on this type of research simply because there are problems may direct to fierce characters and produce monsters to destroy FARE with reasons we do not know why. The argument is there may have evil scientists doing the wrong thing. Religious people say even there are nonsense scientists there are good scientists can figure out methods to demolish those monsters arguments continues without stop. We better ask our Lord God!

At 1000 hour Shania goes to shopping leaving her daughter at home. After half an hour the door bell rings. It is Nadda. Jenny's childhood friend Nadda Laila Lance. Nadda walks into the lounge and sit down. Jenny serves her a cup of multi-formulae spice herb spring water liquid. They talk for a while then suddenly Nadda says,

'Jenny, I heard other people saying you are pretty happy to accompany Rolf. Rolf Vincent Roland. Is it true?'

'Frankly, it is 100% true.'

'Oh! Jenny, don't be silly. Rolf is no good.'

'No good, why?'

'He loves money, power and plays ladies.'

'I don't think so.'

'He is now already having three girl friends. They go out every weekend till late at night.'

'Really?'

'I am not lying. I am not a liar.'

'But Rolf's friends all say Rolf is a good boy.'

'Don't be silly, Jenny. Don't listen to them. We are good friends since infancy. This is not a lie. Trust me, young lady.'

'What contexts make you suspect Rolf is a bad guy?'

'He goes to work every week in a laboratory, doesn't he?'

'My friends told me he is.'

'Actually he goes to ganbling and have drinks with wholf.'

'Does he?'

'Absolutely true.'

'Oh God! Why he does this?'

'Rolf's assessments marks are pretty low because he copies from other students. He copies a bit from this girl and a little bit from another boy.'

'No, this is not true.'

'This is what Rolf told me when I was his guest at his birthday party held in his residency two years ago.'

'Maybe he lied at you.'

'Not really. He laughed happily and loudly when he was saying to me.'

'Are you kidding?'

'Do I look like kidding?'

'I think I am not in the wrong direction, am i?'

'Wow! It is nearly twelve noon. I have to go. Trust me Jenny, absolutely true.'

Nadda leaves then hurrily to Rolf's home address.

Jenny still in puzzle. Did Nadda lie to her?. does Rolf really a bad boy? There is no reason Nadda told her a lie. Rolf and Nadda only met a couple of times and Rolf does not pay attention to her. Is Nadda in the same position as myself such that Rolf hates both of us? Jenny is now in real trouble. Who is able to answer these questions for her? Jenny stays late that night wondering what to do. Will she be happy with Rolf or will she feel secure with Rolf? Jenny's got a problem, a real big problem. Jenny sits at her desk begins to sob again. Oh! Stupid girl, may God has mercy on you!

CHAPTER 9

Good comes Bad goes
Really comes really goes
How come it comes
How go it goes
Who knows God knows

Now no matter what Jenny wakes up which is late for lecture. After lecture Jennifer drives home alone. Jenny is fatigue and feels hopeless, really hopeless. At the same time Nadda is in Rolf's home talking to Kaitar. Nadda chats this and that, gossips and gossips. Suddenly she stops.

'Kaitar, where is Rolf?'

'He goes to work.'

'Oh! Really?'

'Seriously.'

'I don't think so.'

'Why?'

'I think Rolf has gone to a whore's home.'

'Are you kidding?'

'Of course I am not.'

'How do you know?'

'My father knows the whore's friend.'

'How do your father know her friend?'

'Actually the friend is the whore's husband.'

'Are you sure?'

'Pretty sure. The whore Evita and her husband Dong were once arrested under my father who at that time was a police inspector.'

'Don't play.'

'Absolutely not.'

'Oh! Buddha please have mercy on me.'

'It's time to go home. I will talk to you again some time later. Bye.'

Nadda disappear so quick that no one knows where she is. She disappeared as fast as a morning dew. Around 1311 hour Rolf is back home. Rolf is pretty happy that he commence to talk to his Mum as soon as he steps inside the apartment.

'Mum, where are you?'

'I am in bedroom, son.'

'Mum, did you have lunch today?'

'I already had.'

'I have purchased a whole turkey-chicken from Highest-Store-Market.'

'Son.'

'Yes Mum.'

'Did you go to work this morning?'

'Of course I did.'

'Really?'

'Mum what's going on?'

'I was told you go to a whore's house.'

'Who said that?' Rolf is so annoyed he losses his mood for the first time.

'A girl. Your school-mate.'

'Who is she?'

'she is Nadda. Do you know her?'

'Yes for sure. She is an ugly beech.'

'Why did you say that?'

'She always invites me to go out but every time I refuse. About 5 or 6 weeks ago we went out together. She brought me to casino then to stripe-dance.'

'What followed?'

'After that night I did not contact her anymore.'

'Now I understand.'

'As far as I concern Nadda has not come to campus for a fortnight.'

'Why?'

'I do not know why.'

'But how was that?'

'Rumour says she is becoming the hottest prostitute in town.'

'Oh! Jesus, how did it happen?'

'I have no idea. Who cares.'

'But Hadda has only just come to chat with me for a long time.'

'If I am correct. She is not giving genuine information to you, I suppose.'

'Son, you are really genius!'

'Thanks Mum.'

Now, now where is Nadda? She is talking to some undergraduates and PHD students. While she is talking others listen with disproof. They listen and listen and figure how long the speech is going to take. Nadda tries her very best to persuade these students to trust what she is saying. But the audiences have their own idea.

'He is arrogant.'

'How do you know he is arrogant?'

'He used to talk same as giving a speech.'

'Are you giving us a speech now?'

'Of course I am not.'

'He works hard on his assessments.'

'He cheats.'

'How do you know?'

'No, he did not cheat.'

'I am Rolf's supporting witness.'

'He really cheats. Trust me.'Nadda screams.

'He did not cheat, did he?'

'Well! Ah, he never revised his lectures and unfortunately he passed all examinations.'

'That means he did study.'

'Yes, he works hard on his degree. There is no doubt about that.'

'Yes, he even teaches me methods to solve problem questions.'

'Yes, he is so smart he leaves examination room early in every examination and test.'

'No, no, no..... guys. Listen to me. Rolf always asks his senior students for tips before examinations. Do you know that?'

'Rolf does not have friends in year 2 or year 3. How come he got these tips?'

'Well! They come from other Universities, folks!'

'Those students do not know what questions will appear on examination paper, do they?'

'He seek helps from Lecturers in other Universities.'

'Are you kidding? If Rolf actually did it. Are you trying to persuade us to report to authority?'

'He is lazy, always go to play.'

'Now he has returned to as before working hard on his study. everyone knows.'

'He is pretending.'

'He pretends. Well, well ..... he pretends.'

'Rolf always cheats poor people. He is a hypocrite.'

'Sure?'

'Yes. Whenever there is no one nearby he beats young kids for pleasure.'

'You must be Paul A. Keating.'

'Why all of you do not believe in my story?'

'Because you are a skilful liar. This is the core reason, beech!'

'You are defaming Rolf.'

'It is you who is a hypocrite.'

Nadda walks away thinking what to do next. Can she defame Rolf once again in front of Rolf's friends? The only question is --- are they going to trust Nadda? Nadda is thinking, calculating and computing. Then estimate and guess but still cannot sum up a possible solution. It is a bad headache to Nadda.

Now Nadda is going to meet Rolf, by chance on campus. Rolf does not know what Nadda has done to him. Rolf still expect Nadda as a friend. May I ask you Lord to have mercy on this stupid Rolf? Only you, Lord can give him a hand. No one can. Our God always save good-hearted people. This is what God usually does. Now Rolf, God is coming. Thanks Buddha and God!

Nadda is now on campus wandering around. Nadda is not a student. If she is caught by security guards. She is certain in turmoil. Maybe behind bars for 2 years. Does she notice this circumstance?

Today Nadda puts on high heeled shoes to walk for a long time. She is having pain and sore feet makes her cannot walk any further. Nadda the sits on the lawn, takes off her shoes. Let the feet have a break. Nadda is still figuring what methods to attract Rolf. She cannot find out a solution. Obviously, no chances!

Suddenly Nadda sees Rolf walking down the corridor to campus cafeteria. Nadda is so happy that she bursts in tears.
    'Rolf … Rolf …. Rolf….'
    'Hi! Nadda. What a surprise.'
    'Where are you going?'
    'Going home.'
    'You drive?'
    'No, catch an air bus.'
    'Well, I have an companion.'
    'We are not on the same route, I am afraid.'
    'We can stay together until the stop at Light Aerial Tower Exchange, [LATE].'
    'No, it is pretty late.'
    'Oh God! You really have a sense of humour.
    'Anyway let's move on, quick.'
    'Why do you go home early?'
    'To do my business.'
    'What business?'
    'None of your business.'
    'Come on, Rolf.'

'How about you? What are you doing these days?'

'Hanging around.'

'Hang up or down but not around.'

'Well! What are you doing?'

'Looking for a job. You know it is pretty hard to find a job at this time of the year.'

'If you have a certificate it is much much more easier.'

'I am now studying a diploma couse.'

'What's that?'

'Fashion design.'

'Hey! It is a lovely job. It is a dreamed job for most teenage girls.'

'Absolutely.'

'How many more years to go?'

'I have just started.'

'How long is the course, then?'

'Five years if you are lucky.'

'Work hard.'

'I have to get off now. Bye..'

'See you.'

Rolf is a good boy. He is honest and diligent. Rolf does not know Nadda is ruining his future. Rolf also does not know Nadda is doing her best to grab his attention either. Simply because Nadda's bad characters they are not a perfect match. Rolf is intelligent while Nadda is a snake. Nadda tries every single means to destroy Rolf's love affairs and to present a good impression before Kaitar. No matter what Nadda is a nasty snake. No one can stay with her in harmony. At the same time Nadda is convincing other teenage boys Rolf is a naughty boy and to amash all relationships between Rolf and other girls. Evil monster! God's worst creature ever! At the meantime Nadda is not a good student. Late for lectures, not submitting assessments or even talking to students disturbing the Lecturer conducting the lecture. Nadda studies Fashion Design is for fun. It is a winning ticket to marry into a wealthy family. Nadda only lusts for money and power, not to work. Not even a single tiny chore. Is she right? Ask God, please!

CHAPTER 10

Comes comes and comes
Goods goods and goods
Bads bads and bads
You know mate

Besides Nadda there are more problems. People jealous Jenny comes from a rich family. They demolish friendships between Jenny and any other person no matter boys or girls. Jenny has an old friend or let's say an old alien Chardonnay Karen Pacey. She comes from a poor family where her parents were dead at the time she was a teenager. Chardonney is brought up by her grandmother, her mother's mother, whom we all call her Kaka. It relates to chardonney's middle name. This custom is her family's tradition. No one knows why even Chardonney herself and her grandmother. They both live together no relatives. Frankly, the relatives despise their poverty. This annoys Chardonney which let her hates rich people all her life. Kaka once has a younger brother Leon born by his biological mother after his father's third marriage. At that time Kaka is already 32 years old, married and a happy life. Leon is a naughty boy. He always go to gamble that ends up in his bankruptcy to sell his family business. From then on Leon disappear suddenly and secretly. Leon is single no children. Leon takes all family money and flee away. Leaving chardonney's parents Mabel and John work collaboratively. One night John vomited blood and is diagnosed of neurons impairement and malfunction. Because of this incident John commits suicide before his surgery. Mabel also commit suicide in the following morning. Kaka is admitted to hospital for 10 days. Kaka raises her granddaughter despite losing her son and daughter-in-law. It looks like a family tragedy. If all these did not happen what a lovely family they have. They can carry on their business and their study. Now these are fantasies. Similar to a fairy tale. In reality we all have our misfortune. It is our duty to beg Buddha and God to send a Messiah down to earth to direct us in building an Utopia. Can this fairy dream comes to us? Fingers cross!

On this Friday morning Wilson rings to Rolf to invite him to have a cup of coffee at a café round the corner. As soon as Rolf sits down Wilson immediately tells him something excitedly. Wilson discloses on that day the girl spied on Wilson. Yesterday this girl came over to invite Wilson to go out on this coming Saturday night. They will be going to Botanic Garden, Galaxy Zoo then have lunch and dinner together in a five star hotel. Finally at 1915 they are going to watch a show in Television Station LIVE. A perfect arrangement!

This is Wilson's first time in love he doesn't know what to do. What clothes to put on, what topics to talk about and to ask what questions. Her family, her study, her career, her life style or what she loves and hates. What Wilson is going to say about himself. Not to ask what questions that may annoyed her. What can I tell him then? We discuss this all the afternoon. I drink three big cups of coffee that I cannot go to sleep at night.

On Sunday afternoon we meet again in the same café. As soon as we have ordered our food Wilson stirred up a friendly conversation.
    'Rolf, do you know there is an important breakthrough?'
    'Of what?'
    'My relationship with the young girl.'
    'That girl?'
    'Yeah! Her name is Margarita Pech. Yes Margarita Zahra Pech.'
    'Oh! Goodness me. She's got such a name?'
    'What?'

'Not many girls named Margarita, honestly.'

'Are you serious?'

'Not really at this stage.'

'Frankly, her name is a nice name, isn't it?'

'I guess so.'

'Do you know what she told me?'

'No idea.'

'She told me her name, her family and her study.'

'What? This was your first dating, mate.'

'Of course it is. What is the problem?'

'She told you everything?'

'Seriously.'

'Oh! Lord where are you? I lost my way.'

'To tell the truth she invites me to go out every weekend.'

'Is she a girl? Or she only looks like a girl?'

'Rolf, honestly do you encourage me to go on with this relationship?'

'Certainly "Yes"'

'Are you sure?'

'What did she tell you?'

'Her family is not rich. A middle class family which she is the only daughter.'

'What are her parents' occupations?'

'Her mother is a Galaxy History Lecturer and her father is a Mathematician Researcher. Both work in University of Galaxy.'

'What else?'

'She herself loves ocean. Thus, she is a PHD student in Marine Sustainability Development Geobiology.'

'Which area?'

'Both Atlantic and Pacific oceans on earth plus Stormy Ocean in Jupiter and Thunder Rain Ocean in Venus.'

'After you are married you have many diving exercises to learn.'

'even though she prepares to become a Professor she loves a quiet life.'

'Quiet life?'

'Yes, quiet life. She seldom goes out except dinner with family and research conferences.'

'What else?'

'She never shows off. She always works hard hopes to arrive at a breakthrough in her research.'

'Did she do all the talking?'

'She did.'

'What did you say to her?'

'I only said I come from a poor family staying with my mother.'

'Eh …eh ….'

'I honestly have nothing more to say.'

'Did you not?'

'I asked about her research and her study. what motivates her to do this and not much.'

'My God! Where are you? Only these?'

'What else can I talk?'

'You can say anything you like.'

'What?'

'What?'

'While I was talking my mouth was dry. It made me had difficulties on my pronunciations.'

'May God have mercy on you!'

'What can I say?'

'To be honest I have no idea either.'

'What can I do now?'

'Ring her to talk to her and visit her every week.'

'I will do my best.'

'Good on you, mate.'

'I badly need that.'

After this conversation I commence to have a second thought on my relationship with Jennifer. What else can I do at this stage? I do not know how to love her. Meanwhile does she really love me? Honestly I have no idea. Will our relationship continue throughout our whole life. Can we stay together happily with my Mum? Who can say? Can we balance between work and family? Is she going to respect and take care of my Mum same as to her mother? Are we going to lead a happy family? Do we match? Do we understand each other in order to cope with our marriage? The most vital matter is she must take care of my Mum and then there is no divorce. Can she able to do these? God knows!

CHAPTER 11

Smooth seems smooth
Delays seems delay
Good or bad
Bad or good
Together seems separate
Separate seems together
Fight seems assault
Protection seems defence

After this day I have to revise my assessments ready for my graduation examinations. Fortunately, I have not failed in all my units except Gene Pedigree receiving 48.75%. Unfortunately, my appeal upholds then I am ready for my graduation party in June. At this stage my aim is to find a job. What jobs suit me or where I work. I wonder?

Finally I got a job in Sydney West as Genetic Technology Researcher in new human beings, animals and plants by artificial gene engineering. This job is challenging but controversial. The oppose influence is pretty strong. Our FACE government is in a very difficult position to handle this issue. One day Wilson talks to me over Planet-TV-Teleglasses in an extreme serious and worry tone. He tells me some people are working hard to destroy Jenny's future. What methods they manipulate is not known yet. Wilson promises to visit me in the following night. What dirty tricks they are using? I genuine have no idea. I need Wilson tells me the whole story on his visit.

'What are the plots they are going to use?'

'Well it is a nasty plan.'

'What plan?'

'They intend to produce void information to government. Upon these documents Jen will be deporting to another planet.'

'Does it work?'

'I tell you what.'

'What?'

'They release false statements to deface Jen is a secret agent to city council.'

'Jen is not.'

'All of us know Jen is not. We need evidences to clear her name.'

'But how?'

'this is what we are trying to work out tonight.'

'Let me see.'

'Yes?'

'It is simple. We collect evidences to government to prove Jen's innocence.'

'Yes, it is easy.'

'Absolutely!'

'see you.'

'Hey, where are you going, man?'

'I disclose good news to you on my return.'

'All the best, mate.'

'Bye.'

After two months Wilson definitely brings back good news. Wilson tells me Jen is pretty appreciates on my advice and wishes to say "Thank "You" to me. On Friday two weeks later Rolf and Jennifer talk face to face for more than 2 hours under a pleasant circumstance.

On the next day Saturday Jennifer and Rolf go out to picnic hand in hand. They are now in love. Actually they love each other pretty much. Both respect and concern about spouses' parents. From then on these two families live together happily ever after. Fifteen months later a new comer baby girl is born to Jennifer and Rolf and named Kadin.

Love lives
Hate dies
All are true
Truth always live
Truth always alive

03/07/2014 01:47:01
Some stupid ideas about 'Dark Energy'

We all in puzzles of Dark Energy as I watch the education video by Professor from United States on DVD some time ago.

I think dark energy may link or have some connections with Chinese 'Feng Shui' which focus on 'ying' and 'yang' that these two must in balance in order to produce a harmonious environment.

As dark energy seems in everywhere in the globe with enormous potent energy. It is pretty likely the energy, its function, power and impacts are such a large energy that may relate to some other energy or theories not understood at current stage which the theories maybe coming from ancient times or undiscovered civilisations.

INFANCIES TO GREAT GRAND-PARENTS

Since the birth of Universe it is followed by the born of Earth then comes the dawn of civilisations all over the globe. Our ancestors, from any ancient civilisation or ancient empires, at first ate the fruits on the trees. Then began to hunt animals for meals. Gradually, join in groups then communities and nations to go for their different targets. They did what they were told by authorities.

From these events we all know human beings all need to have a working life. No matter rich or poverty we have to also need to work. At our infancy we learn to walk, to talk, and to communicate. All these we imitate our parents, our first attachments, we learn from them. After learning we need to work out the reason they do it and say it repeatedly. We need to do our homework in order to succeed. This is work.

When we grow older up to adolescence we go to school to study. Why we study not go out to play if not with friends we can play on our own. Why? To study is the path to our future work or our dreamed work. We do not study then we do not have sufficient knowledge to work or to satisfied work requirements to fulfil this job. We are then unemployed, no income, no family for the rest of our life. Study is work already. We study hard, we work hard to accomplish to, at least, a pass mark to graduate.

After graduation we join the club to this inhuman society. We find our work then we work hard to support parent, wife and children. Otherwise they all starve to death. We learn the essential knowledge from school is aimed at not commit any crime in our society. Work or study or family all these factors are legally earned and learned and applied. There is a point of discussion. We can learn less in order to work less whenever you hate sit down to study or working in a boring office where the routine works are the same everyday. In spite of these we are still working. The question is the workload pressure is heavy or not. This is also a controversy that workers have diagnosed as they call professional illness.

After marriage our children grown up and we become grand-parents ourselves, at this moment some or most people retired. But we still work. We work in the front lawn or we do housework with our spouse. This is work but lazy work. Still it is work. At retirement we can read books, go to clubs or pubs to have a drink or pursue our hobbies. Reading and drinking are results of our knowledge learned from schools not to participate in criminal activities.

Some people keep working after retirement age. They can resigned from office work go to their hobbies or other careers to achieve their dreams or comply with their hobbies which are set down as desires from infancy. The vocation they hope since childhood. Even God works 6 days and take 1 day break!

What happens if we do not work? It is a big problem! We do not have a job we cannot survive. The biggest worry is your children not willing to study. After schooling they are not eager to look for any job to become a parasite in the society. Of course, you can retire after many years of hardships when you were young. You can relax at retirement to enjoy your life ever after but you already have worked before this moment. 03/07/2014 01:47:01

03/07/2014 01:47:01
Our working brain 1

As we all know human brains transmit signals from neurons via synapses to reach the target destinations. This is similar to radios or television sets receive electronic waves from stations.

Researchers doubted on many devices are used from different neurons. It is because different gestures are sent and decoded by different parts of our body. As our body cells receive these signs the cells will do what is told.

Our brains shrink at adolescence maybe those cells or brain materials are useless and discarded. Just like we have useless codons in our genes. These useless codons were once useful in our ancestors. If we can retrieve these functions again. We have a better chance to find out what happened at the birth of humans or birth of Universe.